Basil Brush
in the
Jungle

Peter Firmin

Basil Brush in the Jungle

Prentice-Hall, Inc.
Englewood Cliffs, N.J.

Copyright © 1970 by Kaye and Ward Ltd.
First American edition published 1979 by Prentice-Hall, Inc.

Printed in The United States of America   J

1 2 3 4 5 6 7 8 9 10

Library of Congress Cataloging in Publication Data

Firmin, Peter.
   Basil Brush in the jungle.

   SUMMARY: Basil the fox and Harry the mole go to
India to find an exotic pet to occupy the cage Basil
has made.
   [1. Foxes–Fiction. 2. Moles (Animals)–Fiction]
I. Title.
PZ7.F49873Bax 1979   [E]   79-15627
ISBN 0-13-066621-1

Basil Brush is a busy fox.
He makes many things in his workshop.

5

He makes things of wood for all his friends.
Once he made a kennel for a dog.

He made a bird-table
for the sparrows, and
he even made a
wigwam for Harry the
mole.

This is a cage that he made of wood.
It was a strong cage, with a lock and
a key, suitable for a wild animal.
"Now we need a wild animal to put
in our cage," said Basil.

"But wild animals live in the jungle,"
said Harry.
"Then we must take our cage to the
jungle," said Basil, "and find a wild animal."

Basil took his money out of his piggy
bank to pay for the journey, and he
called a taxi.
"To the jungle!" said Basil, "where the
wild animals live."

"I will take you to the airport,"
replied the taxi driver.
"Are there wild animals at the airport?"
asked Basil.
"Of course not," said the taxi driver.
"You must take an airplane to India.
That is where the jungle is."

They put their cage on the taxi roof and
drove to the airport. They bought two
tickets to India.

The airplane took them over the sea.
It took them over the forests, over the
deserts and over the mountains to India,
where the jungle is.
It was very hot in India.

Basil and Harry went to a market.
They bought two umbrellas to keep
off the sun.
Basil said to the umbrella man,
"Please tell us the way to the jungle.
We would like to find a wild animal
to put in our cage."

"May I come with you into the jungle?"
said the umbrella man. "I am tired of
selling umbrellas. I will carry your cage."

They walked out of town until they
reached the jungle. They crossed the
river on the ferry boat and sat down to
drink their tea.

"We might catch a crocodile
in the river," said Basil.

Harry threw some cake crumbs into the
water. A crocodile swam towards them.
He ate up the cake crumbs and opened
his mouth for more.
Basil looked at the big teeth
of the crocodile.

"That crocodile would not be happy
in our cage," he said.
"No," said the umbrella man. "It is not
a suitable cage for a crocodile."

They took the cage into the trees.
"We might catch a snake in the trees,"
said Basil.

Harry put some cake crumbs in the cage.
A snake slid out of a tree into the cage.

Harry shut the door. The snake ate up
the cake crumbs, and slid out
through the back.
"That snake is too thin for our cage,"
said Basil.
"True," said the umbrella man. "It is
not a suitable cage for a snake."

All around them were big flowers.
"We might catch a butterfly in the
flowers," said Basil.
"But we have no butterfly net," said
Harry. "Butterflies do not like cake,
they like flowers."
"Then you must pretend to be a flower
in the cage," said Basil.

So Harry pretended to be a flower
and a butterfly flew into the cage.

Harry ran out of the cage and shut the door.
The butterfly closed its wings
and walked out between the bars.

"That butterfly would not have room to
fly in our cage," said Basil.
"No," said the umbrella man. "It is not
a suitable cage for a butterfly."

Harry was angry. He chased the butterfly through the flowers.
He bumped into something furry with stripes. It was a fat tiger.

Harry ran back to Basil.
"Quick!" he said. "I have found
a tiger. Where is the cake?"
"There is no more cake," said Basil.
"That does not matter," said the
umbrella man. "Tigers do not eat cake.
They eat moles and foxes or umbrella men."
"That tiger is too hungry for our
cage," said Basil.

"That's right," said the umbrella man.
"It is not a suitable cage for a tiger.
Let us cross the river before he comes."

They called the ferryboat.
A magpie sat on the boat.
"We might catch that magpie on the boat,"
said Basil, "but we have no cake."

"The magpie is very happy on the boat,"
said the ferry man.

"The crocodile is happy in the river,"
said the umbrella man, "and the snake
and the butterfly and the tiger are happy
in the jungle."

"But I have made a cage of wood,"
said Basil Brush. "It is a strong cage,
with a lock and key, suitable for a wild
animal. I would like to find a wild
animal to put in it."

The umbrella man spoke to the ferry man.
The ferry man spoke to the magpie.
"I promised to help you," said the umbrella
man to Basil. "And the magpie
will help you, too."

"If you go into the cage and show him
the key," he said, "the magpie will
follow you. Magpies like shiny things."

So Basil went into the cage and showed
the shiny key to the magpie.
The magpie snatched the key and gave
it to the ferry man. He locked the door.

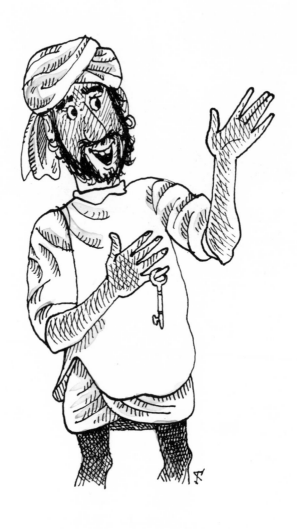

"There you are," said the ferry man.
"Now you have a wild animal in your cage."

"Let me out!" cried Basil. He shook the bars and looked very angry.
It was a strong cage, suitable for a wild animal, and the door was locked.

They crossed the river in the ferryboat
and walked back to the town. They put
the cage on the airplane, and the
ferry man gave the key to Harry.
"Unlock the door when you get home,"
he said. "This fox is too wild for our
jungle."

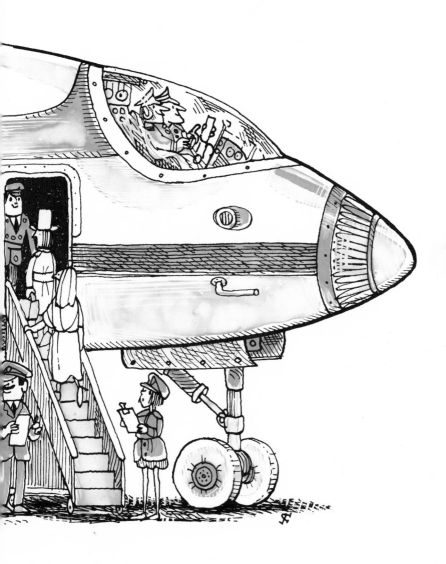

"You know," said the umbrella man, " that was not a suitable cage for a crocodile."
"Oh no!" laughed the ferry man.
"It was not suitable for a snake."
"Indeed no!" laughed the ferry man.
"Nor for a butterfly, a tiger or a magpie," said the umbrella man.
"No, no, no!" laughed the ferry man.

"I'll tell you one thing," said the umbrella man.
"What's that?" asked the ferry man.
"It's a very suitable cage for a fox,"
laughed the umbrella man.

Basil Brush is a busy fox.
He makes many things in his workshop.
Many things…but no more cages.